Noah's Park

PONDER MEETS THE POLKA DOTS

Written by Richard Hays

Illustrated by Chris Sharp

Faith Kids™

A Faith Parenting Guide can be found on page 3.

Faith Kids®

is an imprint of Cook Communications Ministries,
Colorado Springs, Colorado 80918
Cook Communications, Paris, Ontario
Kingsway Communications, Eastbourne, England

PONDER MEETS THE POLKA DOTS
©2000 by The Illustrated Word, Inc.

First printing, 2000
Printed in Canada
04 03 02 01 00   5 4 3 2 1

**Digital art and design: Gary Currant
Executive Producer: Kenneth R. Wilcox**

Ponder Meets the Polka Dots

My child's need: To learn more about forgiveness

Biblical value: Forgiveness

Learning styles: Help your child learn more about forgiveness in the following ways:

Sight: Look at the picture of Ponder as he sits contentedly on his lily pad in the beginning of the story. Then turn to a later picture of Ponder when he's becoming angry at the Polka Dots. Look at his expression. What happens to our faces when we lose patience with others and become angry? Ask your child to think about how it feels when anger is building up inside. How does it begin to affect everything we do, even our facial expressions?

Sound: After you've read the story together, ask your child what lessons Ponder learned in this story. Who reminded him of the example that they received from Noah? What did they all learn by watching Ponder go through his angry feelings? Talk about what anger sounds like in the real world... shouting, yelling, mean words. What can we all do to be kinder to each other?

Touch: Ponder was angry because he thought the purple lily pads were just his, that he had a special right to them and no one else did. Talk to your child about the ownership of things. What things does your child have that he feels are special and just his alone. How would he feel if someone took them away? Would he be able to forgive even if he never got them back again? Ponder discovered once again how important cooperation and sharing and real forgiveness are.

As the sun set, Ponder the frog paddled peacefully around the pond on his green lily pad. The water rocked him gently as he watched the lightning bugs flash. He could hear the snores of Dreamer the rhinoceros coming from Cozy Cave, and Screech the monkey and Shadow the raccoon ch-ch-chattered in the trees above. It was a wonderful summer's eve in Noah's Park.

Ponder smiled as his eyes wandered across the pond. Ever since the big storm had blown away his favorite lily pad, he had started to grow his own. Now there were many beautiful lily pads blooming on the pond. Tomorrow, he would move onto an especially plump, purple lily pad. That one would be his new home.

As he admired the plump, purple lily pad, it started to shake and quiver. It twirled around and then suddenly disappeared with a "pop." Ponder croaked. *Where had his plump, purple lily pad gone?* Now more of the lily pads began to quiver and shake. One by one they twirled around and

disappeared

with a "pop"

beneath the water.

"Help! Help!" My lily pads are being eaten!

My new home is gone!" Ponder shouted.

"Arrrgh!" Dreamer stumbled out of Cozy Cave. "Ponder, I must have had another nightmare. I dreamed that your lily pads were being eaten. That's not a very scary nightmare, though, is it?"

"Something in the pond is eating my lily pads!" screeched Ponder.

"Oh. You're right. There goes another one," Dreamer said, pointing sleepily.

Ponder frantically paddled over to the remaining lily pads. He heard a "crunch." He pulled his paddle from the water. Something had taken a big bite out of it!

Ponder looked into the water.

A pair of lips poked out of the pond and squirted him in the face. Ponder lunged to grab the lips but instead fell headfirst into the water. When Honk the camel saw Ponder fall, he waded in and pulled his friend out of the water.

"They're eating my lily pads!" Ponder sputtered.

"Who?" asked Honk.

"What?" chimed in Dreamer.

"Why?" wondered Screech.

"Where?" questioned Stretch the giraffe.

"How?" inquired Ivory the elephant.

"I don't know who, what, why, where, or how," stammered Ponder. "I only know that I'm going to catch whatever ate my beautiful purple lily pad!"

The other animals watched Ponder floating on his lily pad trying to watch in every direction at once.

"I've never seen Ponder so mad," Ivory said.

"Well, only that one time with Shadow and the fire ants," reminded Honk.

"I wonder what we can do to help him?" asked Stretch.

"Ponder will be all right," said Dreamer. "Remember that he told us that even Noah was angry sometimes."

"What do you think ate the lily pads?" Shadow wondered. "Could it be a giant crocodile with big snapping teeth?"

"Maybe it's a big green snake?" Screech said. "I knew a snake that liked flowers. She picked daisies with her tail."

"I think it's an octopus," claimed Ivory, waving her trunk. "It must have eleventy-two arms."

"Whoever it is, Ponder will figure out how to make friends with it," Stretch said. "Ponder understands the value of friendship."

All that night Ponder guarded the rest of the lily pads. As the sun came up, his eyes drooped shut. His lily pad began to rock from one side to the other. *This is very pleasant*, the tired frog thought. Suddenly, the lily pad shook violently. It began to twirl and spin and dance across the water. Then, with a "pop," it disappeared out from under the groggy frog.

Ponder splashed into the water once more. As he made his way to the shore, he watched all of the remaining lily pads begin to spin and twirl. One by one, they each disappeared with a "pop." There were no more lily pads left on the pond.

Ponder crawled back onto the sand with a grim look on his face. Honk, who had just woken up, looked at Dreamer, who was curled up on the sand.

There was going
to be trouble now.

The next day Ponder asked
Ivory to use her powerful trunk
to help him build a log raft.
"Let's see if these
creatures can chew
through wood,"
Ponder said.

When Ponder and Ivory paddled out on their raft, the other
animals were surprised. They had never seen Ponder so angry.
"Why does it matter? I think that purple lily pad looked like an
eggplant," said Honk.

"Look who's talking," noted Shadow.

"Look," said Howler the lion pointing.

Out on the pond the raft began to rock.

Ponder and Ivory peered over the side of the raft. Splat! Something squirted water in Ivory's face. Ivory squirted back with her trunk. Next something squirted Ivory in the back. She whirled to squirt again and again. "Stop, Ivory! Stop! You're turning the raft in circles!" Ponder yelled at the elephant. But it was too late. Ivory kept whirling and squirting. The raft kept spinning around. Ivory and Ponder were dumped into the pond.

The other animals watched as Ponder and Ivory started to swim towards them. Suddenly, several big fins popped out of the water. They began to circle the frog and the elephant.

"Ivory! Ponder! Look out!" cried Shadow from the shore, "Sharks! Sharks!"

Ivory spun around. They were
surrounded by the big fins.
Were they really sharks? Ivory grabbed
Ponder and threw the frog to the shore.
He landed on his behind with a thump.
Then she swam as fast as she could until she, too, reached
the shore safely. This time, though, the creatures
from the pond followed. The animals now saw
what was eating Ponder's lily pads.

They were not sharks or crocodiles or octopuses with eleventy-two arms. They were just fish, though probably the strangest fish any of the animals had ever seen. The fish were covered with polka dots of every color.

"Well," said Honk with a smile, "they certainly do look dangerous. In fact, they are the most dangerous creatures I have ever seen."

Shadow and Screech rolled on the ground with laughter.

"They may not look dangerous, but they have eaten all my lily pads," said Ponder, rubbing his lower half, "and caused pain in other areas as well."

Ponder turned to the funny-looking fish.

"You are not welcome here. You must leave the pond and Noah's Park."

The other animals looked at each other.

"Wait, Ponder. You can't just throw them out," said Dreamer. "You told us that Noah learned forgiveness from God. Shouldn't you forgive these fish?"

"Maybe they didn't know that you were going to live on the lily pads," added Stretch.

Ponder looked at his friends and shook his head. "No, they must leave," he said, "or I will."

The next day Ponder paddled out on the raft. He stopped in the middle of the pond and sat quietly. After a few minutes, the polka-dotted fish began to swim around the raft. They swam around and around. Still Ponder did not move.

After a while, one of the fish popped out of the water. This one had pink and green polka dots. "Good afternoon, frog. I am Gobble, the leader of the polka dots. We have decided to move on. Thank you for the use of your pond. The lily pads were delicious, by the way."

"Why did you eat them?" asked Ponder. "They were mine. I was going to live on the plump, purple one."

Gobble laughed, "Lily pads are our favorite food."

"You attacked us, too," said Ponder.

Gobble shrugged. "We weren't really trying to hurt you.
It is just the way we are. It is our nature. We like to squirt
things, and we love to eat lily pads. Many creatures
do not like us. Well, thank you again.
You do have a very nice pond."

Ponder watched as the polka dots began to swim away. He turned and began to paddle back to the shore. After a few seconds he stopped paddling. *Dreamer and Honk were right,* he thought. *Noah would have forgiven the fish and loved them as neighbors. Noah was forgiving of others as God had taught him to be.* He quickly turned around. "Wait, Gobble!" he called. "Come back! You can stay!"

Later that evening, Ponder asked Gobble, "If I grow more lily pads, do you think we can share them?"

"Perhaps," nodded Gobble, "but we might eat them all anyway. They are very tasty."

"You are very hard creatures to like, but at least you are honest. I guess the raft will have to be my home. You won't eat it, will you?" said Ponder.

"We'll leave the raft alone," laughed Gobble. "Too many splinters anyway."

"I think I will learn a lot from you, Gobble. What would you think if we called the pond, Polka Dot Pond?" Ponder smiled.

Gobble just laughed, but forever after that the pond was known as Polka Dot Pond.

The End

DREAMER HAS A NIGHTMARE

Dreamer the rhinoceros loves to dream, until one day he has his first nightmare. How will Dreamer handle this frightening experience? Discover the answer in the Noah's Park adventure, *Dreamer Has a Nightmare*.

STRETCH'S TREASURE HUNT

Stretch the giraffe grew up watching her parents search for the Treasure of Nosy Rock. Imagine what happens when she finds out that the treasure might be buried in Noah's Park. Watch the fur fly as Stretch and her friends look for treasure in *Stretch's Treasure Hunt*.

CAMELS DON'T FLY

Honk the camel finds a statue of a camel with wings. Now, he is convinced that he can fly, too. Will Honk be the first camel to fly? Find out in the Noah's Park adventure, *Camels Don't Fly*.

DREAMER AND THE MYSTERY OF COZY CAVE

Dreamer the rhinoceros loves to dream. One day he dreams that there is a secret passage in Cozy Cave and then discovers it is real. He and his friends set out to explore the passage. Will they discover the mystery of Cozy Cave? Find out in the newest adventure from Noah's Park, *Dreamer and the Mystery of Cozy Cave*.

HONK'S BIG ADVENTURE

On the first day of spring, all the animals of Noah's Park are playing in the mud, water, and leaves. This good clean fun creates a lot of dirty animals. When Honk the camel sees the mess, he decides to leave Noah's Park and find a clean place to live. Will Honk find what he searches for? Find out in the hilarious Noah's Park story, *Honk's Big Adventure*.